W9-BST-854

GAME FACE

Chasing the Baton

by Rich Wallace
illustrated by Tim Heitz

Calico

An Imprint of Magic Wagon
abdopublishing.com

abdopublishing.com

Published by Magic Wagon, a division of ABDO, PO Box 398166, Minneapolis, Minnesota 55439. Copyright © 2016 by Abdo Consulting Group, Inc. International copyrights reserved in all countries. No part of this book may be reproduced in any form without written permission from the publisher. Calico™ is a trademark and logo of Magic Wagon.

Printed in the United States of America, North Mankato, Minnesota.
092015
012016

THIS BOOK CONTAINS RECYCLED MATERIALS

Written by Rich Wallace
Illustrated by Tim Heitz
Edited by Heidi M.D. Elston, Megan M. Gunderson & Bridget O'Brien
Designed by Laura Mitchell

Extra special thanks to our content consultant, Scott Lauinger!

Library of Congress Cataloging-in-Publication Data

Wallace, Rich, author.
  Chasing the baton / by Rich Wallace ; illustrated by Tim Heitz.
    pages cm. -- (Game face)
  Summary: It is track season and seventh-grader Marcus is struggling at the 400 meter distance and upset that his best friend Torry jokes about his slow times--so he is determined to build up enough strength to earn a place on the 4x400 meter relay at the upcoming track and field meet.
  ISBN 978-1-62402-133-6
1. Running races--Juvenile fiction. 2. Relay racing--Juvenile fiction. 3. Best friends--Juvenile fiction. [1. Track and field--Fiction. 2. Running--Fiction. 3. Best friends--Fiction. 4. Friendship--Fiction.] I. Heitz, Tim, illustrator. II. Title.
  PZ7.W15877Ch 2016
  813.54--dc23
  [Fic]
                          2015024881

TABLE OF CONTENTS

ONE

Slow Motion

Eight pairs of spikes *click-click-clicked* on the red rubber track. Eight runners churned legs and arms, rushing along the backstretch. My teammate Adam was just inches ahead of me. I thought he would have left me in the dust by now. Not today!

Adam and the other eighth graders demolished me in most of the workouts. But halfway through my first middle school race, I was on the verge of a win. I could feel it.

Kick hard, I told myself as we rounded the turn. *You've got this!* Less than 200 meters to cover now. In half a minute I'd be done.

I reached deep for more speed. *Blow past these guys!* But suddenly I had nothing left. My legs were turning to jelly and my arms were as heavy as cement. Why was I running in slow motion?

Somehow I fought through the turn and onto the straightaway. I looked up toward the finish line, but I couldn't see that far. What I could see were the other runners pulling away. The next-to-last runner was 5 meters ahead of me. Adam was out of sight.

"Finish strong, Marcus!" yelled my friend Torry Santana. "Kick!"

But I wasn't sure if I could finish at all. There would be nothing strong about it, that's for sure.

My shoulders were tight. I could taste the chili I'd had for lunch—about to come up. I was wobbling from side to side and the finish line was still 50 meters away.

Finally I crossed it. I closed my eyes and leaned over, hands on my knees, puffing hard. Last place.

Torry ran up to me. "Great start!" Then he lowered his voice and grinned. "Horrible finish."

I straightened up and looked around. I could barely see the bleachers, but I knew my dad was up there. I coughed up a wad of spit. "Where's our stuff?"

Torry pointed to a pile of orange-and-blue sweats on the infield.

I fumbled in a pocket for my glasses, and suddenly I could see.

"It must be hard to race when you can't see where you're going!" Torry said.

I forced a smile. "I can see well enough to stay in my lane."

I don't like sprinting with my glasses on. For sports like basketball and soccer I wear protective goggles, but running isn't much of a problem. "I just wish nobody else had seen it. I got trounced!"

Coach Parrish tapped me on the shoulder. "Not bad for the first time, Thorpe," he said. "You went out way too fast, but you'll learn. The 400 is all about pacing."

I nodded. "Pace and pain!"

Coach grinned. "I never said it was easy." He turned and hurried to the finish line, as the next race was beginning.

I flopped onto the grass and yanked off my spikes. "I don't get it," I said. "We've been training for three weeks. And I was already in good shape before that. I thought I'd finish near the leaders, but I was a long way from being the best. I was so far out I couldn't even see the winners. How did I wind up last?"

"You were right with 'em halfway through," Torry said. "You'll get stronger."

"Wish I were a sprinter like you," I said. Torry had placed fourth in the 100-meter dash. "There's barely enough time to get tired in a race that short," I told him. "Boom! It's over before you know it."

"Ha!" Torry replied. "It still hurts."

"For about two seconds."

Torry shrugged. "A little more than that. But yeah, it's not like the 400."

"I don't think there's anything like the 400," I said. "Wish I could drop down to the sprints."

But Bethune is loaded with fast sprinters. Coach had convinced me to move up to the longer event, where speed and endurance are equally important. Torry is

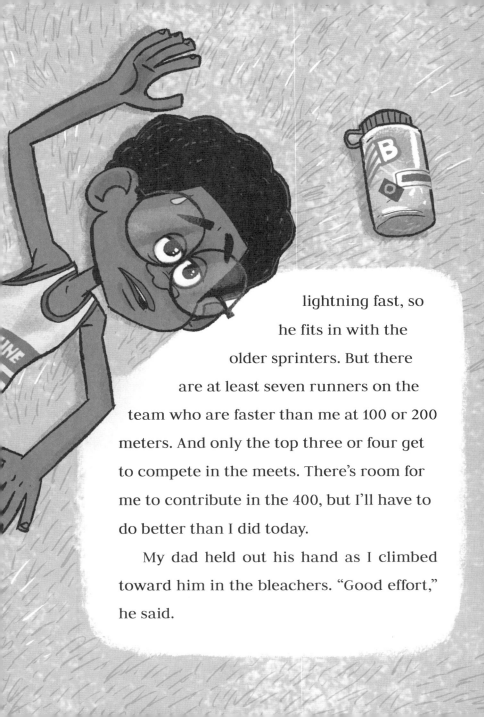

lightning fast, so he fits in with the older sprinters. But there are at least seven runners on the team who are faster than me at 100 or 200 meters. And only the top three or four get to compete in the meets. There's room for me to contribute in the 400, but I'll have to do better than I did today.

My dad held out his hand as I climbed toward him in the bleachers. "Good effort," he said.

That made me wince. Dad didn't say great race or anything like that. Good effort sounded almost like a put-down, although my father never would have meant it that way. He's always supportive, whatever I'm trying.

I plunked down on the metal bleachers, which were nearly empty. Just a few parents were watching the meet.

"My effort wasn't the problem," I said. "I ran out of gas. Don't know how I even finished."

"Everybody ties up at the end of a 400," Dad said. "You just tied up a little sooner than the others."

"*Way* sooner. I was barely halfway done. That's when the monkey jumped on my back."

Dad laughed. "I never ran track—baseball was my springtime game—but I knew a lot of people who did. The trick is to ration out your speed. That way you have enough energy left for a strong finish."

"That's what Coach keeps saying." I squinted and stared at the track, where the hurdlers were racing toward the finish line. "It's easier said than done."

"Experience is everything in sports," Dad said. "Run a bit smarter next time. Little by little, you'll see a difference."

"I hope there is a next time. Coach could easily replace me."

"Then you'll prove yourself in practice. Look, that kid Adam, who won the race? When you hit 200 meters, he was only half a step ahead of you. But he beat you by 30 meters. Speed wasn't the difference. Endurance was."

"Yeah. I stay pretty close to him when we run shorter distances in practice."

"See?" Dad said. "You're as fast as a rabbit, but you have to learn how to use that speed."

I shook out my wrists and took a deep breath. "I need to jog. Otherwise I'll tighten up."

"You're done racing for today?"

"Yeah. There's no way Coach would put me on the relay after that disaster."

Four runners would team up for the 4x400 meter relay, the final event of the meet. Even though I'd been the third fastest for Bethune in the 400, there were several others who would be chosen for the relay before I was. Some sprinters and hurdlers were faster at the 400, even though it wasn't their primary event.

So after I cooled down, I watched the relay with Dad. The race was close until the anchor leg. Adam grabbed the baton from Oscar and quickly opened a lead. He broke the tape at the finish line with a 10-meter lead.

"That could be you next season," Dad said.

"Maybe." I was a long way from being that strong. Like an idiot, I tried to sprint the entire race today, even though I knew that was impossible. I'd been running on fear instead of intelligence. I didn't want to fall way behind and be embarrassed. But it had turned out like that anyway.

"Next time," I muttered.

Dad squeezed my shoulder. "There's always a next time," he said. "That's the great thing about sports. It might take eight or ten 'next times' before you get it right. But when you do, it'll be sweet."

TWO
Against Myself

"Nice way to start the season," Torry said as we left the field and walked toward home. "With a win."

I wanted to feel good about that, but I hadn't contributed anything to the team's victory with my last-place finish. Torry had added a third in the 200 meters to his fourth in the 100. And our friend Griffin scored a point with a fifth-place finish in the shot put.

We'd have five more meets like today's, with three or four teams going head-to-head each time. After that would be the league championship meet for anyone who qualified. I'd have to run at least six seconds faster to have any shot at competing in the league meet.

"I don't see why you two want to run so much," said Griffin, who's a lot bigger than either of us and as big as most of the eighth graders. "In any other sport, the coach makes us run as punishment. If you don't hustle in basketball, you run sprints. If you mess up in soccer, you run laps. Why would you volunteer to run all day?"

I knew he was joking, but it was a good question. After today, I didn't have a good answer.

"Racing is pure," Torry said. "No teammates to help you out except by yelling at you. It's just me against the other racers. Me against the stopwatch."

"Felt like it was me against myself today," I said. "My legs betrayed me."

"I saw your race," Griffin said. "You looked . . . let's see, I'll try to put it gently. Awkward?"

I let out a deep breath and pictured myself on the final straightaway. I had used every ounce of strength, but it was a losing battle.

"Torry's right," I said. "You're totally on your own out there in a race. And believe me, it feels pretty helpless when the other runners are leaving you in the dust."

"Join the shot putters!" Griffin said. "We put up a lot of dust."

"I'm too scrawny for that." I picked up a shot put

once. It was heavy. I couldn't imagine throwing it very far. "I'll stick with the 400. For now."

"Did you hear about that relay race coming up at the high school meet?" Torry asked.

I didn't know what he was talking about.

"Next Friday night," he said. "Under the lights at the high school stadium. They're having a big relay meet—at least a dozen schools—and they scheduled one middle-school race."

Sounded exciting. Maybe we'd go watch.

"You could be on that team," Torry said.

"How?" I asked.

"It's a 4x400. You're a 400-meter guy, right?"

"Yeah, but I can think of at least half a dozen people Coach would pick before me."

"It's ten days away. That's forever. You can move up," Torry said.

"I doubt it." I tugged at my backpack straps.

"I might try to get on that team myself," Torry said. "That would be so cool. Running under the lights in front of a packed stadium. Everybody in the bleachers watching me soar past the other runners."

It did sound cool. The exact opposite of what happened to me today. But maybe I could redeem myself. Maybe . . .

"No relays for me," Griffin said. "Not unless I can throw the shot, pick it up, throw it again, and keep at it until I do a whole lap. Bet neither one of you could beat me at that."

When we got to Griffin's street, he turned off toward his house and we headed for ours. I live right across the street from Torry. Our dads own an accounting business together, and we've known each other since we were babies.

I've usually been a step or so behind Torry in sports, but I like the challenge of going one-on-one in basketball or bike races or anything else we come up with. I'm a good athlete, but with Torry around I'm never best at anything.

Lately we've been hanging out a lot with Griffin and another friend, Javon Park. Javon's playing baseball this spring, but we're hoping he'll switch to track next year. He's fast, too.

"Seriously, are you going to try to get on that relay?" I asked.

"Seriously, yes," Torry said. "You too. Why should it be all eighth graders?"

"It's twice as far as you're used to racing."

Torry shrugged. "Our group runs 400s in practice sometimes. I can handle it. I heard there'll be a run-off trial during a workout. Anyone who wants one gets a shot at it. Top four make the cut."

I started to smile. Maybe I'd get to see Torry in the same predicament I'd been in. Overconfidence is dangerous in a long race.

I was starving. "See you tomorrow," I said, heading up our walk.

"Don't wimp out of the trial," Torry said. "Maybe we'll both get in. How cool would that be?"

After dinner, my dad and I played our usual game of chess. I told him about the relay.

"Coach hasn't said anything about it, but one of the assistants mentioned it to Torry," I said as I moved a bishop into striking position.

"Sounds like a great opportunity," Dad said, calmly taking my bishop with a knight that I hadn't been paying attention to. "Next Friday night? I'll be in Chicago most of the week for a conference. Might not be back in time."

I'd forgotten about the annual accountants' conference. It was Dad's turn to go this year. Torry's father went last year.

"I'm not thinking about the relay," I said, even though I was. I pushed a pawn forward one space.

Dad studied the board, then moved his rook sideways four spaces. "Check."

This game was going about as well as my race. I protected my king with the other bishop, which left Dad with an easy shot at my queen. I winced, but there was no going back after making a move. Even a bad one.

Dad took the queen and grinned at me. "You're not concentrating."

"Too much on my mind." I tilted over my king, conceding the game.

Mom poked her head into the den. "Is he going too hard on you, Marcus?" she said with a laugh.

"Never," I replied. I shook my head and stared at the board, replaying the last several moves to figure out what I'd done wrong. I smiled, too. "It's very instructional, getting demolished like that every night," I joked. "Builds character, right Dad?"

He'd told me that a few times. But honestly, I'd never want him to let me win. I got over that ages ago. Winning one game in fifty is okay by me since I know I earn it when I do manage to beat him.

I guess that's why I won't give up on the 400 either. Like he said, it'll be sweet when I finally get it right.

THREE

Worth Celebrating

It had rained earlier in the day and the grass was damp, so I sat on the track to stretch before practice. "Not sure why we do this," I said to Torry. "I'm always stretchy."

"Coach says it can help prevent injuries," Torry replied. "But me too—I'm like a rubber band."

I'd checked the workout posted in the locker room. My group would be doing a "ladder" today, beginning with an easy 200-meter run and climbing to a 600. Then we'd work our way back down the ladder, increasing our speed on each repetition.

That was the theory anyway. It looked tough. I figured I'd be hanging on for dear life by the end. But I needed a hard workout to build strength. I never want to finish a race the way I did yesterday. Ever.

Coach blew his whistle. "Let's have the 400 group here!" he called.

I hurried over and joined Adam and four others at the starting line. I took off my sweatshirt and hung it on the fence, then checked my laces. No track spikes in practice, just my regular running shoes. My feet are big for my size; Dad says I'll grow into them and be as tall as he is.

"Half a lap," Coach said. "Nice and smooth, like it's the first part of a race." He looked at me and nodded, as if he was singling me out. "Pace yourselves."

I felt a surge of energy but knew I couldn't spend it all at once. *Ration it out*, I told myself. *Finish as strong as you begin.*

Adam shot into the lead. I settled into third, just behind Oscar, who'd finished second in yesterday's meet. Both of those teammates are taller and more muscular than I am. They eased through the half lap and slowed to a jog. I stayed close, but I was putting out more of an effort than they were. Still, it felt easy.

"That was a little too slow," Coach said as we returned to the starting line. "Try to match that pace for this entire 400. Be consistent."

I swallowed hard, remembering the pain from yesterday's 400. But I'd run that same distance dozens of times in the past few weeks without so much trouble. I was just too excited yesterday. Too eager.

"Go!" Coach yelled.

Hold back, I thought. I dropped to the end of the pack, easing around the turn and onto the backstretch. Adam and Oscar already had a big lead, but I didn't care. I wasn't jogging, but I wasn't going anywhere near as fast as I had yesterday.

At the midpoint, the leaders were 15 meters ahead of me. I swung into the second turn. I was breathing hard, but my muscles weren't tightening up like they did in the race.

I finished last, but I gained on a couple of runners on the straightaway. And Adam was only 20 meters ahead this time.

"Jog a full lap to recover," Coach said. He waved me over to him. "Don't be timid. You can run harder than that."

"I was trying to pace it out."

"Good. But you still have to move."

I *was* moving.

When I caught up to the others, Adam turned and asked, "What did Coach want?"

"He just told me to work harder."

Adam laughed. "Coach never thinks any of us are working hard enough. Get used to it!"

The others were bunched up, so I jogged a few yards back. At the start of the season, even these jogs between harder runs had been a chore. Now I barely felt them. I could run all day at this pace.

"Track!" came a call from behind.

I leaped sideways off the track as a group of sprinters raced by. Torry was up with the leaders, who were all a head taller than he was.

"Stay there!" I yelled. "Relax!"

Torry didn't look back, but he lifted his hand and gave a thumbs-up, never losing his steady rhythm. Torry's a natural runner. Actually he's great at every sport. But he works hard at it, too, so I don't feel *too* envious.

Coach is always reminding us to jog in the outside lanes so we don't get trampled. There were four groups from the boys' team and as many from the girls' squad running reps today. It can get crowded!

"Anyone hear about that relay in the high school meet?" I asked.

"Coach mentioned something," Adam said.

"Should be a trial next week to decide who'll compete, just like last year," Oscar added.

Those two had nothing to worry about. There was no way Coach would leave them off the relay. I didn't plan to worry about it either. I wouldn't be on that team.

"This time, 600 meters," Coach said to us. "A lap and a half. Again, I want to see a steady pace throughout. Don't just jog and kick. You shouldn't be straining, but you should be on the edge, working hard."

Oscar took the lead this time. The pace was slower, and I dug in behind Adam. I usually beat the other members of the group—two seventh graders and one eighth grader. But I knew that any of them could take my spot in the lineup. They'd all beaten me once today, so I hung close to Adam for the entire first lap.

"Relax and keep driving," Coach said as we passed him with half a lap to go.

I glanced back. The other three were a few yards behind.

"Don't look back!" Coach called. "That's wasted energy."

I know that, but it's hard not to peek.

I felt good, and I stayed a stride behind Oscar and Adam until they finished. Big difference so far today.

But now I faced another 400.

Coach had said that the first three runs shouldn't be much more than an aggressive warm-up. But this second 400 should feel like a

race. And the closing 200 should drain any strength we have left. And there shouldn't be much.

"That's how you build," Coach said. "Hard day, easy day."

"I thought yesterday was hard," I said.

"Nah. Meets are easy." He winked. "Sometimes."

Ha! Let me know when that happens!

So here was my chance to replay yesterday's race. There was no reason to hold anything back now. If I dropped out of the top three, I might lose my lineup spot.

"Run smart," was all Coach said. He blew his whistle and we took off.

We didn't have to stay in lanes today, so we were bunched tight on the first turn. As soon as we hit the backstretch, Adam and Oscar sped up. I moved into third, but I knew better than to stick close to the leaders. I'd paid that price yesterday, and I wouldn't do it again.

Not yet, I told myself at the midpoint. I planned to hold this pace until the final straightaway, then go all out. I could hear the others breathing down my neck, and sensed one swinging wide to try to pass me. I stuck to the inside to make him work.

We reached the homestretch and Dante pulled even. There was none of that tightening I'd felt yesterday. It hurt, but I didn't seem to be slowing down. We raced side by side to the finish line, and I managed to out-lean him.

Dante reached out his hand and I slapped it. He's an eighth grader and we're evenly matched, but I've been edging him most of the time lately. "Great job," I gasped.

"You too," he said.

Coach looked at his watch. "Hey, Thorpe!"

"Yeah?"

"You ran three seconds faster than yesterday."

That was news. I'd run faster and it felt easier!

"You were about a second and a half slower at the midpoint. See what I mean about pace? You had plenty left, so your second 200 was almost five seconds faster than yesterday."

I nodded, hands on my knees. It sure wasn't easy, but that was my fastest 400 ever. Worth celebrating, except for one thing.

"Take a nice long rest," Coach said. Then he laughed. "Like seven more seconds. Line up!"

We all groaned.

"Hold on, Coach," Dante said. "What's this rumor about a middle school relay at the high school meet?"

Coach shook his head. "Focus on this workout." He tooted his whistle and we ran.

Adam, Oscar, and Dante got a big jump on the rest of us. I was sixth again as we reached the backstretch, but this was it. The last 100 meters of the workout.

"Run 'em down!" came a familiar voice. Griffin was at the side of the track, carrying a shot put and heading toward the locker room. That was all the urging I needed. I passed the other seventh graders and zeroed in on Dante.

I caught him but couldn't pass him. He finished inches ahead. But I was back on track. Yesterday's race already felt like the distant past. Today had definitely provided forward momentum.

FOUR

Challenged!

"You're not done yet?" I asked Torry. I was surprised to see him still in his shorts and tank, hopping up and down at the side of the track. I'd been finished for ten minutes. Dressed and ready to walk home.

"I need to take a few jumps," he said. "I'll be done soon."

Since Torry's a runner and a jumper, he has to do double-duty in practice. I walked to the edge of the long jump pit to watch.

He was a blur from where I stood. I only saw his bright red shirt sprinting up the runway.

But as the runner approached, I realized it wasn't Torry at all. The jumper soared over the sand and landed with a whoosh!

"Great jump," I said.

"Thanks, Marcus," said Tanya Clark. She brushed the damp sand from her knees and stood next to me. Tanya's in my science class and we were on a soccer team together a few years back.

"I finally hit the board on that one," she said. "Took about eight thousand jumps to get it right."

"I guess that's why we practice."

"If I could have jumped like that yesterday, I would have won the meet," she said. "Instead of placing sixth."

"Sixth isn't bad."

Tanya leaned in and whispered. "I got beat by two girls I out-jump every day in practice. That never should have happened."

"Sounds like we both had a tough first meet," I said. "I rigged up bad in my race."

"Saw it," Tanya replied.

"Yeah, I guess everybody did."

She smiled. "Hard to miss."

Torry unleashed a powerful jump and landed about six inches farther than Tanya.

"Mark that spot," she said, pointing to the sand. "I'll beat it." She ran along the grass back to her starting point on the runway.

"One more jump for me," Torry said. "Then we can leave."

Tanya extended her legs even farther on her next jump, straining as she landed an inch farther than Torry's mark.

I poked Torry in the shoulder. "Challenge!" I said. "She beat you."

"Not done yet," he said.

"I am. Even if he beats me," Tanya said as we waited. "Let him pretend he's better, just for one night."

Torry jumped about six inches farther than before, but he came up frowning. "I think I fouled," he said. "Felt like my toe was over the end of the board when I took off."

Tanya held out her hand for him to slap. "We'll call it even," she said. "Just to be nice." She winked and jogged toward the locker rooms.

"Wait a minute," Torry said. "Don't be 'nice.' One more jump apiece, no?"

Tanya stopped and rolled her eyes. "Okay, chump. Guess I'm up first."

I nudged Torry. "What happens if she beats you, Torry?"

"If she beats me, she beats me. Tanya's an awesome athlete."

She jumped about the same distance as before. I drew a line in the sand with the end of the rake.

"Are you running that relay?" Tanya asked me as we waited for Torry to jump.

"Don't know." I didn't even know for sure if there was a relay. But everybody else seemed to think so.

"Nothing's going to keep me off that team," she said.

Tanya's a sprinter, but I had no doubt that she could run a fast 400. She'd probably be the fastest one on the girls' team. Her older sister is a big star on the high school squad.

I watched the take-off board to make sure Torry didn't foul. He hit it square and soared several inches past the line in the sand.

"Good one," Tanya said. "Something for me to shoot for tomorrow."

"Me too," he replied. "I think that was my best ever."

I told them that I'd run faster in practice today than I had in the meet.

"Everybody ran faster than that!" Torry said. He took some very slow steps and acted like he couldn't lift his arms. "Look at me, I can't finish!"

I folded my arms, turning away. "Very funny."

"I'm just busting you, bro," Torry said.

I knew that. We bust each other all the time. No hard feelings. Plus, I could tell he was showing off for Tanya, so I tried to let it go. But that comment stung a little more than usual.

"Look," I said, "I'm heading for home. Otherwise I'll be late for dinner."

"I'll be five minutes," Torry said.

"I'll be halfway home by then." I started walking. "See you in the morning."

"Two minutes? I've just gotta get my stuff from the locker."

I kept going. "See you later."

I walked fast because I didn't want him catching up to me. I had felt really good about the improvement I made today. I needed to reclaim that feeling.

Instead of heading down Harrison Street, I cut over to King. That way, Torry wouldn't find me even if he did speed up. It was hard not to feel bad about avoiding him, but I did it anyway.

Torry is the most competitive person I know. But he's almost always supportive. We make fun of each other constantly. Usually it doesn't hurt at all.

Let it go, I kept thinking.

I thought about the difference between today and yesterday. It wasn't just that I'd run faster. I'd done it after running three reps already: 1,200 meters of running. All because I ran smarter.

Our next meet wasn't until Monday—five more days. I figured we'd have a lighter practice tomorrow, then Coach would run us into the ground on Friday. I needed to keep proving that I belonged in the lineup. I was exhausted now. Dinner. Homework. Sleep.

I reached Prospect Avenue just in time to see Torry cross from Harrison, running as fast as if he hadn't used any energy today. He was probably running to find me, but I hung back and let him go. He didn't see me.

I sat on a bench by the bus stop and waited a few minutes, just in case he stopped by my house. I wasn't mad. Not really. Just didn't feel like talking to him.

I focused on my next race. But then I kept thinking about the one that might happen after that. The time trial for the relay. I wouldn't pretend that I could win it, but top four? That might happen.

And if big-mouth Torry was in the race? Well, maybe he'd think twice about mocking me after I trounced him. Until then, I'd keep my distance from him.

And I did, too. On Saturday afternoon I headed over to Griffin's house to play some video games.

"Where's Torry?" Griffin asked when I arrived.

"I don't know," I said. "He wasn't around." I didn't tell him I hadn't bothered to check.

"Video basketball is better with four," Javon said. "He knows you were coming over, right?"

I shrugged. "Sure." But I hadn't said anything to Torry. Javon and Griffin just assumed that if I went somewhere, Torry would, too.

"He'll show up," Javon said. He fiddled with his game stick. Javon is the shortest one of us, but he always takes the role of a seven-foot center when we play a video basketball game. "Torry would never miss a chance to beat us at anything, including these games."

But when Torry arrived an hour later, he said he'd been waiting for me at home. "Why didn't you come by?" he asked.

"I thought you'd already left to come here."

"Why would I do that?"

I changed the subject and we played the game. But I wasn't in the mood for it. They were all joking around, and Torry was acting like he was some big sports star. "Coach said as soon as I figure out how to hit the long jump board at full speed, I'll probably break the school record," he said.

I hardly said anything the whole time. After two rounds I told them I had to leave.

"You just got here," Javon said.

"My parents said to be home early. We're supposed to do something."

"You running home or walking?" Torry asked.

"I'll probably run," I said. "It'll be good practice." It was only a few blocks though.

"Don't run too fast," Torry said.

"Why not?"

He broke into a grin and did that same slow-motion action with his arms. "So you'll be able to make it all the way."

Javon and Griffin laughed. I smiled, but I couldn't wait to get out of there. I sprinted all the way home.

My parents were out doing yard work.

"Home so soon?" Mom asked.

"Yeah. I was bored with the games. Didn't feel like sitting still."

"We're going to jog in a little while," Dad said. "Want to join us?"

"Sure." I started up the steps.

"Marcus?" Mom said.

"Yeah?"

"Is everything okay? You're getting along with your friends?" Mom asked.

"Yeah. Why?"

"You've spent more time alone the past few days. And I thought you'd be at Griffin's all afternoon."

"I'm tired of video games," I said. "No, everything's okay."

I couldn't wait for Monday's meet. Nobody'd be making fun of me after I ran the best race of my life.

If I ran the best race of my life. I might tie up just as bad as last time. But that's a chance you take in sports. My dad always says you'll probably lose more times than you win.

Unless you're Torry, who always seems to triumph.

My parents jog every day, but they're usually too slow for me. I wanted to save my energy for Monday though, so a nice easy pace was perfect. We ran past my school and along Main Street, then circled back to our house.

"Another mile?" Dad asked as we stopped in the driveway.

"Not for me," Mom said. "You two go ahead."

Being with my father always makes me feel good. He's a calm guy, and he towers over me, so I still feel like a little kid with I'm with him. That's okay. At twelve, you're always being told to grow up and act like a man. Sometimes I just want to be a kid, especially when my friends have been acting like jerks.

"You've been quiet," Dad said after we'd run two blocks.

"Yeah. Lots to think about."

"Racing? Or something else?"

"Mostly racing," I said. "How I measure up."

"You're measuring up just fine," Dad said. "Remember, you've been competing against guys who are older than you, and you're in a very tough event that takes seasoning."

"Torry's the same age as me. He's one of the top runners already."

"He's an exception," Dad said. "But you can catch up to him. Hard work pays off."

We reached the edge of town and Dad stopped running. "Let's walk back."

"Okay."

"I think this is about more than 'measuring up,' isn't it?" he said. "Is somebody giving you a hard time?"

"Not really," I replied. "I was just a little embarrassed about that first race. I got kidded about it some."

"That happens."

"I'll handle it," I said. "On the track. Can't wait."

Dad put his hand on my shoulder. "That's the way," he said. "Move on. Get better. However long it takes."

I nodded. Athletic success seemed to come so easy for some people. I knew I was a good athlete. But competing against great ones was very humbling.

"Track's tough," Dad said. "If a guy is faster than you are, then the only thing you can do is outwork him."

"What if the guy is faster and works as hard as you do?"

Dad laughed. "Let's not worry about that, all right? Sports should be fun. Don't ever lose sight of that."

FIVE

Hard As Ever

I was so excited for Monday's meet that I wore my orange jersey under my shirt at school. But my excitement dropped like a rock when I ran into Dante between classes.

"Coach said I'll be running the 400 today," he told me.

"Great," I said, trying to sound enthused for him. But where did that put me? Coach wouldn't leave Adam or Oscar out. Looked like I might not be competing at all.

"Will there be two sections?" I asked.

"Not sure," he said. "Probably not. There are only three teams, so two or three guys from each."

That math didn't sound promising. Coach said there would be two heats in some of the bigger meets. But it didn't sound like this would be one of them.

So I felt miserable all through my morning classes. I'd been waiting almost a week to redeem myself. When the bell rang, I hustled down to the gym to see if Coach had posted a lineup.

Relief! Our 400 runners for today were Oscar, Dante, and me. Adam was listed in the 800 instead.

I stared at the list for a minute to make sure. Then I sprinted up the stairs so I wouldn't be late for my next class.

The afternoon seemed to take forever, but finally it was race time. I shook hands with Dante and we lined up.

"Runners take your marks," said the official. I closed my eyes and breathed deeply, imagining my finish. Last week the final 50 meters had felt like a mile. Heavy legs, heavy arms, heavy breaths.

I leaned forward and brought my right arm back. I was out in lane 7, so the only opponent I could see was in lane 8. He was taller and looked fierce in his maroon and silver EASTSIDE jersey.

"Set."

Get out fast, I thought, *but not too fast!*

We charged forward, racing around the first turn. Since we had to stay in lanes for the entire lap, I did my best not to be concerned with anyone else. I'd know where I stood when we hit the second turn.

Relax. Stay fast, but save something for the end.

Our teammates yelled as we reached the backstretch. "Stay with them!" called Torry. I let my shoulders relax. Held a steady pace.

Oscar was in lane 4, and he and the guy next to him pulled even with me as we neared the turn. That actually meant that they were ahead, since the lanes are staggered. I did my best to maintain their pace.

We hit the halfway mark. This second turn was crucial. I had to hold it together.

We came off the turn and we still had 100 painful meters to go. Oscar was leading a tight pack of three up front. Dante, in lane 1, was a half meter ahead of me. Everyone was breathing hard. At least it wasn't a runaway this time.

Drive, Marcus! Drive!

The race was a blur now. It hurt just as much as last time, but I wasn't slowing down as much. I passed the Eastside runner in lane 8 and stumbled across the line. Had I beaten Dante for fourth? Too close to tell.

"Great run!" Torry yelled, holding out his palm.

I barely touched him. Oscar patted my shoulder as I dropped to my knees.

"Big difference today," I said, still panting. That last 100 meters had been as hard as ever. But I had held it together a little longer before the crash started.

I jogged for a couple of minutes, then headed into the bleachers to see my parents.

"Much better today," Dad said. "You looked a lot smoother on that second turn."

"Thanks."

"You were just over a minute," he said. "Much faster."

That's pretty good. The qualifying time for the league meet is 59.5. I can get that.

"Could you tell if I beat Dante?" With him in lane 1 and me in lane 7, it was hard to tell. Not to mention I hadn't been wearing my glasses.

"He nosed you out," Mom said. "Not more than a tenth of a second, I'd say."

Dad checked his watch. "I'm cutting it close. Need to get to the airport. I'll call late tonight when we land."

Mom handed me a water bottle. The day was hot and I was sweating heavily. We paused to listen to the announcer.

"Hey, I scored!" I said. Fifth place was worth one point. That was as good as Torry had done in the 100.

"That's worth celebrating," Mom said. "Since it's just you and me tonight, maybe we'll get a pizza."

"Great."

"Do you want to invite Torry over?"

Usually that would be a sure thing, but for once I hesitated. "I'm kind of tired. Maybe not this time."

My Bethune teammates dominated the rest of the meet. Adam won the 800, although he'd told me this might be the only time he ran that event all season. If that was true, it would be between me and Dante for the third spot in the 400-meter lineup. Right now, Dante had the advantage.

We stood to watch the 200-meter race. Even with my glasses on, I couldn't see the other side of the track clearly. But I could pick out my teammates' orange jerseys. Torry was over there somewhere.

"Go, Torry!" my mother yelled.

Several racers were even as they came off the turn. I could pick out Torry now, and he was right with them. In fact, he was beating all of the Bethune runners.

"Go, go, go," Mom said. She wasn't yelling now. It was almost like she was talking to herself.

The top three runners leaned at the finish, with Torry among them. I couldn't tell who won, but Torry had run the best race of his life.

"Not bad for a seventh grader," Mom said.

I nodded. He was definitely fast.

I watched as Torry and the others bunched up around the officials. Torry leaped into the air and let out a whoop. The others looked disappointed.

"He won!" Mom said. "Incredible."

Our teammates gathered around him, patting his back and yelling.

"I'd better go down there," I said. "I'll see you at home, Mom."

I grabbed Torry's shoulder and told him he was awesome. All four runners who'd beaten him in the 100 had also been in the 200, so it was quite a comeback.

We won the meet handily. Coach called a team meeting in the locker room.

"Great job," he said. "I think we can go undefeated this season if we keep working at it."

Torry waved his hand. "Coach?"

"I know what you want to ask," Coach said with a smile. "Friday night is the Twilight Relays, a big tradition in this town. There's a middle school 4x400 relay again, which hasn't been much of a secret.

"I was waiting until after today's meet to explain. Anyone who wants to run the trial, be ready at the start of practice on Wednesday. We'll go a little easier tomorrow, but not much."

I did a rundown in my head. Adam and Oscar seemed certain to earn spots on the relay team. Dante had edged me today. Torry looked like a world-beater in that 200, so he'd be very tough to beat, even in a longer race. There were at least three others who were as fast as me or faster.

It wouldn't be easy. But why should it be? I'd definitely be out there trying.

SIX

On Trial

Griffin, Javon, and Torry were at a corner table in the cafeteria when I got there Tuesday. I'd spent a few extra minutes at my algebra class, grilling the teacher about an equation I didn't quite understand, so they already had their lunches.

Good excuse for sitting somewhere else.

I got in the lunch line and tried to decide between chicken nuggets and sausages. I'd opted for the chicken when someone tapped me on the shoulder.

"Tanya," I said. "Nice work yesterday." I hadn't had a chance to congratulate her on her pair of second place finishes in the long jump and the 100.

"Thanks. Really looking forward to tomorrow."

I just nodded.

"The relay trial, remember?"

I gave half a laugh. "No need to remind me. It's keeping me up at night."

"Really? I think it'll be fun."

"Maybe." I hoped so. "Fun isn't exactly the right word for it."

"Inspiring?" she said. "Awesome?"

"That's closer. Where are you sitting?" I asked.

"Anywhere." She jutted her chin toward Torry. "I'll join you guys over there."

She took the last chair, so I pulled one from another table and squeezed between Javon and Griffin.

Torry and Tanya started talking about their jumps, which was fine with me. I still didn't feel like Torry and I were square. Maybe after tomorrow.

"Did you get on the field yesterday?" I asked Javon. He's a pitcher and an outfielder, but he hadn't played an inning in the first couple of games.

Javon shook his head. "Carlos blew the save in the bottom of the last inning. Wouldn't have happened if Coach had brought me in instead."

"He has no idea what a star he has on the bench," I joked.

"Right," Javon said. "I'm this hidden talent. I haven't thrown a pitch all spring. Coach always favors the eighth graders. I know they have reputations, but that doesn't mean results."

I sipped my juice. "I keep telling you, track's different. If you out-run or out-jump the other guy, the coach has to give you a chance. Performances don't lie." That was another thing to love about track. And to hate about it. "You should switch over next spring," I told him.

"I might do that," Javon said. "Love baseball, though. Besides, next year I'll be an eighth grader. It'll be my turn."

"You can get your turn in summer ball, too," Griffin said.

"Yeah, but that's two months away. For now I'm stuck riding the pine in the dugout."

Griffin said, "See? The seventh graders get no experience. So when they're eighth graders, it's like they're being thrown to the wolves."

"Tell me something I don't know," Javon said with a sigh. He lifted his hands to shoulder height and smiled. "All this talent, going to waste."

"All that food, too," I said, stealing a nugget from his plate. Javon hadn't eaten a single bite. He'd been too busy talking as usual.

He looked up at the clock and frowned. "No more discussion. Eat!" He started inhaling the rest of his lunch.

I popped my last nugget into my mouth and wiped my hands with a napkin. "Have a good practice," I said to Javon. "Hope you don't spend all of it sitting down."

Dad sent me an e-mail from Chicago.

Good luck tomorrow. You don't need luck, but you know what I mean. Can't wait to hear about the trial. Wish I could see it.

I wrote back with a joke.

Maybe it'll be on the TV news. Seriously, I'm nervous!

I didn't hear back right away, but I figured he was in a meeting. So I worked on my algebra, which was almost as big a challenge as track. At least tonight's assignment didn't take too long.

Before bed, I checked my e-mail again. Dad had written back.

Every runner in the race will be just as nervous as you are, even if they don't show it. Pressure like that makes athletes do odd things. Even the best can fold when the going gets tough. So just relax, run smart, and ENJOY IT. Love you. Good night!

I printed the message and stuck it in my math book so I could read it anytime I needed to tomorrow. Then I stretched out on my bed and stared at the ceiling.

Visualize, I told myself. It was as if I were watching myself run the race, figuring out the spots where I could relax just a fraction and where I needed to go all out.

You'd think picturing myself racing would get me keyed up. Instead, imagining a sprint calmed me down. I saw myself holding it together on the homestretch this time. Tiring out but not tying up.

I took a deep breath and let it out. I was ready for sleep. Ready for anything.

Even ready for the toughest race of my life.

I hoped.

"It's like the Olympic Games," Torry said as we jogged the infield before the trial. "All or nothing."

I didn't need "all." Just a spot in the top four. But there were a lot of us warming up and only eight lanes. We'd have to run in two sections and compare the times.

Torry kept talking, but I ignored him. I never want any distractions when I'm preparing for an event.

It was the warmest day so far this spring, but that didn't bother me at all. The sun felt great, loosening my muscles. I took a sip of water and shut my eyes. I was ready for this.

"I guess Friday's meet will be the Olympics," Torry continued. "Today is more like the Olympic trials." He raised his arms and leaned as if he was breaking a finish-line tape. "World champion."

Don't be too sure, Torry, I thought. He'd run the 400 in practice a few times, but never in a race. That final straightaway might give him a rude awakening. Or maybe not. Torry always seemed to pull through in the big events. He belonged in this trial. Did I?

Spikes today. Top speed.

I leaned against a hurdle and watched Tanya win the girls' trial by 5 meters. Then I carefully folded my glasses and tucked them away. I could taste sweat at the corners of my mouth.

Coach called us over with surprising news. "Adam and Oscar," he said, "sit this one out. You've both earned a spot on the team for Friday."

I did a quick count of the other runners. Eight of us. One section. Two relay spots.

I needed to beat either Dante or Torry, for sure. Two eighth graders—Jake and Sergio—usually ran on the relay, too, and they'd be in the thick of this one. Coach put them in lanes 4 and 5—center of the track. Dante was in lane 3 and I took 6. Torry was just outside of me in 7.

I inhaled deeply and shook out my legs.

"Good luck, guys," said Sergio, a hurdler and jumper. His times were about a second faster than mine, but I'd been coming on strong in the past week. I was ready to run faster.

Eight days ago I finished last in my first track meet. Today—with Adam and Oscar out of the race—I was hoping for first.

Torry hopped up and down a few times. Sergio blew his breath out hard. I just stared straight ahead.

"Take your marks," Coach said.

I tried to relax.

"Set."

I shivered slightly, despite the heat.

Tweet! At the blast of the whistle, I burst forward, leaning into the curve.

Torry was moving fast. He was at least 2 meters ahead of me before we reached the back straightaway, and I could sense Sergio just off my shoulder.

Steady, I thought. *Long way to go.*

Sergio drew even, then forged ahead. Torry was several strides in front, and Jake and Dante moved into my side vision.

No need to panic. It was good to know where everybody was. Could Torry maintain that pace? Could I?

We reached the midpoint. My spikes dug into the track, which had softened in the heat. *Here's where the fun starts*, I thought.

Torry glanced back. He knew better than that. He had a few meters on me, but we were running at the same pace now.

Middle of the turn. The spot where I'd rigged up last week. I was straining. We all were. You could sense it. Other than Torry, we were bunched so close I could have reached out and touched Dante, Jake, or Sergio.

Griffin and some others were clapping in rhythm at the head of the homestretch. I heard Adam and Oscar yelling.

I dug down. Whatever I had left, I needed to spend it now. Fourth place. Not good enough. Ninety meters to go. *Dig, Marcus. Dig!*

Dante broke first, falling behind. Torry's hands were slicing at the air, his shoulders stiffening. Sergio and I were in lockstep, fighting for an advantage. I had nothing left. Or did I?

We'd cut Torry's lead in half. Sergio was inches in front of me, our feet hitting the track simultaneously, our elbows nearly colliding.

Twenty meters from the finish line, we drew even with Torry. I heard his gasping, heard my own groaning.

I surged. I leaned. I beat Torry! He fell to the track and rolled across my lane.

Sergio grabbed my arm. "Great race," he said.

"Who won?" I puffed.

Sergio shook his head and choked out some words. "I think I got you. But not by much. Doesn't matter. You and I are on the team!"

That was hard to believe, but it was true. I looked at Torry, down on his hands and knees on the infield, looking miserable. I knew the feeling.

But this feeling was so much better!

Coach said we'd need to be at the high school no later than six o'clock on Friday even though we wouldn't race until eight o'clock. Oscar was assigned the leadoff leg, then Sergio, then me. Adam would be the anchor, as usual.

"Torry," Coach said, "you're the alternate. Be dressed to run, just in case."

"Who are we running against?" Oscar asked.

"Not sure," Coach replied. "It'll be a full house, though. Expect very strong competition. Every school's best. But you can do this."

Torry sat quietly and listened. I'd been very psyched up to beat him, but I wasn't going to rub it in. He'd given every ounce of energy, just as I had. My little bit of experience at the longer distance had made a huge difference.

I nudged him with my elbow.

"Congratulations," he mumbled. "You earned that."

"Yeah, I did. You made it tough, though." I had to respect that. Every time I've beaten him at anything, it took maximum effort to do it.

But this was definitely a switch. I couldn't remember beating him at anything when the stakes were so high.

Torry stood up. "Back to work," he said, shaking out his arms.

I'd forgotten that we still had a workout ahead of us. But Coach had promised that it would be a light one for anyone that made the relay team. In two days we'd be racing again, and we'd be in a big-time spotlight. Full crowd. High school coaches watching.

"Should be an easy day," I said.

"Not for me," Torry said with a frown. "I'm going harder than ever. Never gonna let that happen again."

Let what happen? Getting beat by me? Is that such an insult? Maybe he thought so.

I was tempted to do his "running in slow motion" action like he pulled on me last week. But I kept it to myself. "It's all good," I said. "The harder we work, the better we get."

Torry stared at the track for a moment. "You go easy today," he said. "I want to see you fully recovered for Friday, bro. Race of your life."

"There'll be lots more."

Coach blew his whistle. Torry jumped into the next rep with the sprinters. I lined up with Adam and Oscar and Dante and waited for instructions.

I knew I belonged here now.

SEVEN

An Unwanted Rivalry

"I made it, Dad!" I blurted as soon as he picked up the phone. I told him everything about the race. How I outran Torry.

"Fantastic! I've got a five o'clock flight out of Chicago on Friday," he said. "I should be back in time for the race if everything goes smoothly."

"Hope so," I said. I was already getting nervous. Walking home I'd pictured myself on that third leg. If Oscar and Sergio ran well, I might get the baton in the lead. The pressure to not fall behind would be intense.

I've been to football games in the high school stadium when the place is rocking. Bleachers full, spotlights brighter than daytime, all that energy focused on the field. For one minute or so, every pair of eyes in the stadium would be on me—the guy carrying the stick for the home team.

"You'll do great," Dad said. "You're as fast as a rabbit, remember?"

I swallowed hard. "A scared rabbit." Then I laughed. "A fwightened widdle wabbit."

"Let me restate that," Dad said. "You're as fast as an antelope. How's that?"

"Cool." Dad always makes me feel better. Sure hope he can get to Friday's race.

"How did Torry take it?" he asked.

"All right, I guess. He doesn't like to lose."

"No kidding."

"But . . . he especially doesn't like losing to me. He acts like that's a huge letdown."

"I get it," Dad said. "Don't worry. He'll figure out soon that losing a close one to you should feel like an honor. You've got to realize that too, Marcus. You're a better athlete than either you or Torry realizes. He's just used to being the star."

"He always has been."

"Things change. Talent takes you a long way. Hard work takes you further."

At dinner, Mom grilled me about Torry. She could tell that I'd been avoiding him, and that had never happened before. Living across the street from Torry was like having a brother. We did everything together.

"It's too bad you and he didn't both make the relay team," she said. "You'd feel like teammates again instead of rivals."

I picked at my pasta and veggies. I was hungry, but somehow I didn't feel like eating. Part of it was nervousness about Friday. Mom was right about the other part. I missed hanging out with Torry.

"Yeah," I finally said. "We got forced into being rivals. That won't last, I hope."

Mom glanced out the window when we heard a *thump thump thump* in the driveway.

"You've got a visitor," she said.

Torry was shooting baskets out there. The Santanas have a basket, too, of course, so why was he over here?

"He obviously wants you to go out," Mom said.

"He could knock on the door."

"Get out there."

I gulped my last forkfuls of pasta and put on my sports goggles.

"Be nice," Mom said.

"I always am."

I swung open the back door and stepped onto the deck. Torry was dribbling with his back to me, but he knew I was out there. Still, I figured I could speak first.

"What's up?" I asked.

"Thought you might want to shoot some hoops," he said, not looking over as he sank a lay-up.

"Sure. Not one-on-one, though. We've gotta save our legs."

"I don't race until Tuesday." He bounced me the ball. "Just some H-O-R-S-E. You go first."

"Let me warm up." I shot a 10-foot jumper, then banked the ball off the backboard from a few feet out. I made both shots. "Okay," I said. "Ready."

I wondered if letting him win would ease some of the tension. But he'd sense that immediately and demand I test him. Besides, I never had to let him win at anything. He took care of that himself.

I stepped to the free-throw line with my back to the basket, leaned back, and tossed the ball over my head. It swished.

"Man, what is it, your birthday?" Torry said. He missed the shot.

I sank a fifteen-footer. He missed the follow-up. Torry's a great shooter, but I couldn't miss tonight. Even when I took ridiculous shots like a running left-handed hook. We were both laughing after I made that one, which was a step in the right direction. I won easily, only reaching *H*.

We sat on the back steps for a few minutes. I wasn't sure what to say. We watched the red lights of a jet cruise past, way overhead. "That 400 is tough, no?" I finally said.

Torry nodded. "Sure would like to run it again, though, on Friday. That's such an amazing opportunity."

I stretched out my legs and leaned back. "Adam ran it last year. Said it was the coolest event he'd ever been in. Took home bronze."

"Make sure it's gold this time."

"I'll do my best."

He spun the basketball on his fingertip, then stood and dribbled it through his legs. He bounced it hard, chased it down, and sank a lay-up after a behind-the-back carry.

"Pretty good," I said.

"For an alternate."

"That's better than nothing," I said. "Like my dad says, you put in the work, you earn the results. Your dad says that, too."

"Every day," Torry replied. "At least twice today. I know all about that. I'm just not used to this."

"Not getting what you want?"

"Yeah. But it's okay. It just inspires me to work harder. After that trial today, I did the hardest workout of my life. A few more of those . . ."

I nodded. I definitely knew what Torry was capable of.

"I have to get in," he said, looking toward his house. "Thanks for the game. Second thrashing of the day."

"It happens."

"This one didn't hurt so much," he said, breaking into a smile. "See you in the morning."

I stayed on the steps, staring at the sky. I had homework to do, but I wasn't ready to go in. Sometimes I just like to sit in the night with my eyes closed, letting the breeze cool my skin. It helps me think.

Tonight I thought about everything I'd accomplished in such a short time. From last place to a spot on the relay team. Not too bad. And it looked like Torry and I were all right again.

But what would happen Friday? Another breakthrough or the big rig?

I'd find out soon enough.

EIGHT

Chaos and Confusion

Coach held up a relay baton before Thursday's practice. He slapped it into his palm and grinned. "Handoffs," he said. "Bad ones can cost you a victory. Let's work on them."

I'd never run a relay before, so I hadn't given much thought to passing the baton. But we had to do it at top speed, with as little fumbling as possible, while keeping our balance and avoiding collisions with the other runners.

It's easy to foul it up. Especially if you can't see very well. But it's part of what makes a relay so exciting.

Coach had us jog a few laps with the baton, getting a feel for running with it and trying some handoffs. Oscar handed it to Sergio, then Sergio to me, then me to Adam. It wasn't difficult to do at half speed, but I anticipated trouble when we sped things up.

I was right. Coach pointed to the starting line where I waited for Sergio, who sprinted toward me from 10 meters away. "Stick!" Sergio called. I reached back, but I'd barely started moving, and Sergio ran into me as I tried to grab the baton.

"You have to be running at the same speed as Sergio," Coach said. "Too fast or too slow and you'll mess it up. Try again."

I took off too soon this time, and Sergio couldn't catch up. I had to slow to nearly a stop, which totally killed our momentum.

We went through that a dozen times. Then it was my turn to sprint, handing the baton to Adam. That went a lot smoother, since Adam's experience told him when to move and how fast.

"Not bad," Coach said after we'd been at it for twenty minutes. "It's much harder in a race with so many teams, though. As you'll see."

He called several other runners over, filling five lanes of the track about 25 meters back. Coach gave them batons and set us four relay members plus Torry at the starting line: Adam in lane 1, Oscar in 2, Sergio in 3, me in 4, and Torry in 5.

"Here's the twist," Coach said. "Adam, you're taking the baton from the runner in lane 4.

Marcus, your teammate is in lane 1." He mixed us all up like that.

"That's how it is in a race sometimes," Coach said. "In the scramble down the homestretch, runners pass each other and shift from lane to lane. Your job"—he pointed to us—"is to move into the best position for the baton pass. You don't want to be reaching over another runner or getting tangled up when your teammate is trying to hand you the stick. At full speed, of course!"

Our first try was awful. My teammate was in second place as he ran toward the finish line, but I couldn't get around Sergio or Oscar quickly enough. I was last by the time I scrambled over to him and grabbed the baton. It didn't help that I hadn't seen him clearly until he was nearly to the finish line.

"It's all right to be physical, Marcus," Coach said. "You can't shove your opponent out of the way, but you can move around him. You have to move around him sometimes. If he's in the way, push past."

We tried it again, with a different mix of lanes. My elbow smacked into Oscar's as I tried to take the pass, and the baton fell to the track. Torry tripped over Adam's foot. Coach blew his whistle.

"Not good," he said. "It probably won't be quite so crowded in the meet, by the way. The runners will be spread out more by the time you've gone a lap or two. But we need to be prepared for chaos. It happens."

We switched roles. Now I was sprinting up the track, trying to outrun Adam and the others while also looking for my teammate.

Did I mention that my vision isn't good? Finding the right guy in a mass of five wasn't easy.

"On Friday, everyone will be in uniform, so the colors will help," Coach explained.

I hoped no other team would be wearing orange.

We worked more on handoffs, without the stampede of so many runners. Just Sergio passing to me, then me passing to Adam.

"Look," Sergio said, "unless I happen to have a big lead, I'll be sure to stay at the edge of lane 2 on the homestretch. As long as you're near that spot, I'll find you."

"Same thing for me," Adam said. "Be in lane 1 if you're in the clear, but drift out to 2 if other runners are crowding you. And I'll wave my hands overhead, so you'll have something to look for."

"Man," I said, "racing 400 meters is hard enough. Now I need to be a navigator, too."

Sergio asked how many teams would be racing.

"I think every lane will be taken, so probably eight. The first leg will stay in lanes, so that pass should go smoothly. But you have to be ready for some jostling on the other exchanges."

It occurred to me that I'd do better running the leadoff leg. But Coach said he needed a faster guy there to get us out near the lead. Third leg was the safest spot for me, since most teams would put their slowest runner there. For our team, that was me. Oscar, Sergio, and Adam were all faster than me, so far.

So I was the only one who'd have to make two treacherous exchanges. As the leadoff runner, Oscar would only have to pass once. Sergio would take the baton from him while still in a designated lane. And after Adam took the pass from me, he'd finish the race.

Didn't seem like a great placement for me, since my eyesight was a liability. But Coach was set on that lineup. I'd have to live with it.

"Let's keep at it," I said. I definitely needed more practice.

Walking home, Torry suggested that I could wear my sports goggles during the relay. "It'll help you with the exchanges," he said. "If you can't see who you're passing the baton to until you're almost on top of him, you're bound to mess it up."

"Maybe I can get away with my regular glasses," I said. "I'll just wear a tight strap. The goggles aren't really necessary. It's not like I'll be getting smacked around like in basketball."

"We'll practice in the driveway tonight," he said. "I'll figure out something to use as a baton."

I still didn't like the idea of going full speed in my glasses. But it seemed like the best option, especially after all that confusion this afternoon.

So we ran through it a few times after dinner. I borrowed one of the eyeglass straps that my mom uses when she plays tennis. It would take some getting used to, but the strap held my glasses steady while we passed the baton. Torry and I did a quick run around the block, too, to make sure the glasses didn't wobble.

"That works," I said. "Good suggestion."

"That's my contribution to the relay," Torry said. "That and my big mouth. You'll hear me yelling every step of the way."

I called Dad again and filled him in on everything.

"Sounds like you and Torry have worked things out," he said. "Glad to hear it."

"We didn't say anything about, you know, why we weren't getting along," I said. "It just seems to have eased up. I think he respects me more as an athlete now."

"Good for him. And you. I'll drive straight to the stadium from the airport tomorrow. I should be there on time."

"Mom said she'll video it."

"Sure, but I want to experience it in person," Dad said.

"Me too." I laughed. "I mean, I wish I could sit in the bleachers and watch myself run."

"That would be some trick," Dad said.

At bedtime I checked my track shoes, making sure each spike was tight and secure. I neatly folded my orange jersey and the blue shorts. My uniform was all set for tomorrow.

Was I?

NINE

Lightning Quick

There was no practice for us on Friday afternoon, so I went home for an early dinner. Mom teaches kindergarten, so she's usually home by the time I get there. I wanted a very simple meal: a turkey sandwich, some fruit. Nothing I'd be tasting during the race.

Torry knocked on the door before I'd taken a bite. "Ready to go?" he asked. He was wearing his sweats and carrying his spikes. Just in case.

I looked at the clock. "We don't have to be there for an hour," I said. My dad was getting on a plane in Chicago, I hoped.

"I can't wait," Torry said, doing a silly dance.

"Shoot some baskets. I'll be out in a minute." I got my ball out of the closet and tossed it to him.

I was glad to see so much enthusiasm from Torry for a race he wouldn't be in. I figured most of our team would be watching from the bleachers. That was motivation, for sure.

The high school parking lot was full of school buses from all over, and hundreds of athletes were warming up when we arrived. The high school races were scheduled to start at seven o'clock.

We looked around and tried to spot any middle school teams we knew. The Eastside crew was sitting in the bleachers. I recognized the guy I'd edged on Monday.

This was way bigger than the two meets I'd been in so far. There were dozens of officials in yellow vests, and the bleachers were filling quickly with spectators. I smelled hot dogs and french fries from the refreshment stand, and music was playing from the announcer's booth.

Coach called us over to a spot near the long jump pit. He held up a program.

"Eight schools in our race," he said. "Oscar, you'll be in lane 2. There are some strong teams listed."

I was sweating pretty hard, even though we hadn't warmed up yet. Nerves, I guess. The night was warm with a nice little breeze. Perfect conditions.

"Take a long, easy warm-up," Coach said. "And pay attention to the high school races. Watch the exchanges—you'll learn something. And listen for the announcement to check in for your race."

Adam appointed Torry as chief listener, since he wouldn't be running. Torry saluted and said, "Count on me, General."

It occurred to me that I hadn't said one word since we'd arrived at the stadium. My voice squeaked when I tried to speak. I tried again. "Do we get numbers?" I'd noticed that most of the high school kids had numbers pinned to the front of their jerseys.

"Yep," Coach said. "I'll hold them a while longer."

The numbers looked very official and big-time. Good souvenirs.

"Can we keep them?" I asked.

"Sure," Coach said. "Pin it to your bulletin board. But a medal would be better. Top three teams get 'em."

The announcer called for sprint relay teams to check in. A big pack of high school runners trotted along the track, some of them carrying starting blocks. I felt puny compared to them.

"Are we going to have muscles like that in a few years?" I said to Torry.

He flexed his biceps. "I'm halfway there," he said. But he isn't any bigger than I am.

Their speed was even more impressive. It was a one-lap relay. Each man ran only a quarter of the distance—100 meters. But the baton passes were lightning quick, and the power of the runners

was amazing. They were like trucks going by at full speed.

The girls' race was just as impressive.

"Where's Tanya?" I asked. "That was her sister who won the race."

"She's up there with the rest of the team," Torry said. "She'll be ready."

I looked up toward the bleachers but couldn't single anyone out.

"See my dad?" I asked.

Torry looked. "No, but I'm sure he's on his way."

We're only twenty minutes from the airport, so if he'd landed on time he'd get here. We were still about a half hour away from race time.

The announcer called for another event, then added, "If you aren't in the next race, please leave the track and the infield."

"Let's go," Adam said. "Numbers, spikes. Time to get ready."

We jogged along the edge of the parking lot, practicing handoffs and encouraging each other. A team in yellow-and-green sweats jogged past in the other direction. They looked close to our age.

"Middle school?" Adam asked them.

The biggest guy stopped and said, "Yeah." He had a beard! Not much of one, but yikes. I didn't have even the hint of facial hair yet.

Their uniforms said HILLSDALE. That's like an hour away from here. If they came this far for a race, they must be good.

I swallowed hard and stared at the guy's beard. His three teammates were all about nine feet tall. What do they feed them over in Hillsdale?

"Good luck," their leader said. "See you on the track."

We jogged some more.

"Big," Sergio said.

"No matter," Adam replied. "They weren't here last year though. I have no idea if they're any good."

We heard the announcement to check in for our race. That did it. Suddenly I felt like I might throw up. My sweat turned cold. I wiped my face with my sleeve and slowed to a walk.

Adam hustled to the starting line to check us in. I took a deep breath and shut my eyes. No backing out now.

I felt really alone and scared.

Then I felt a hand on my shoulder.

"All you can do is give it your best," Dad said.

I let out my breath and smiled. Dad held up his fist and I bumped it with my own.

Now I was ready to do this thing. The excitement returned. I jogged to the track and found my teammates.

"Let's go, guys!" I said. "Let's win this."

TEN

Final Kick

We were up next, but the race underway on the track had all of our attention. Everyone in the bleachers leaped to their feet, screaming as the anchor legs barreled toward the finish line. Four runners were locked in a tight race, straining with all their energy. They leaned at the tape.

The winner jumped with his baton held high and his teammates swarmed him.

I looked at Torry. "Couldn't have been closer."

"Awesome," was all he said.

The announcer called attention to us. "Next on the track is the middle school 4x400. Some future stars in this one, no doubt."

We smacked Oscar on the shoulder and he stepped over to lane 2. I read the jerseys of some of our opponents: KENNEDY. LONGMEADOW. ST. MICHAEL'S. None of them were orange, but I was still glad I had my glasses on.

Torry put both hands on my shoulders and squeezed. "Think gold," he said.

My mouth was dry. My hands were shaking. I hopped up and down. "Too late for the alternate?" I said.

"No wimping out," Torry replied.

"Just kidding," I said.

I wanted this.

I stepped around a runner from the previous race, who was lying flat on the grass, moaning. His teammates helped him up, and he limped away across the field.

"Take your marks," said an official, holding his starter's pistol in the air.

I bounced a few more times and then the runners burst from the line as the gun fired. A collective "Wooooo!" rose from the crowd.

In less than two minutes I'd be out there running. In three I'd be done.

"Do it up, Sergio," I said softly as he stepped onto the track to wait for the stick. Oscar looked very smooth on the backstretch, but all eight runners were fast. It was hard to tell who was leading.

"Looking good," Torry said. He turned to me. "Gonna be interesting."

"Gonna be brutal."

They reached the homestretch. Sergio raised his arm, looking intense. The Hillsdale runner had a clear lead in lane 5, but Oscar and two others were inches apart.

"Kick!" I yelled as they ran past us.

There was lots of jostling at the handoff, but Sergio took a pretty smooth pass from Oscar and cut toward the inside lane.

Eastside moved into second place on the turn, and Sergio settled into third.

"Get out there," Torry said, giving me a gentle shove. I checked my eyeglass strap. Made sure my shoelaces were secure.

This is really happening, I thought. I pushed between two others, taking a spot at the edge of lane 2, as we'd planned. Inside of me was the Eastside kid I'd beaten on Monday. The Hillsdale runner with the beard was on my other side. He looked like he should be the anchor instead of the third leg, but looks can be deceiving.

I couldn't see clearly, but it appeared that two or three runners had caught up to Sergio. Another stampede to the finish line. *Pass somebody*, I thought. *Give me a clear shot at the handoff.*

As they reached the homestretch, I squinted and looked for orange. The leaders were packed tight, fighting for position, but Sergio must have fallen behind. I couldn't see him with the leaders.

The bearded guy stepped around me and nudged me with his shoulder. I could see green and yellow in front, so he belonged there. Another runner moved behind me and squeezed into my lane, forcing me farther out.

Here they came. Hillsdale took off, then Kennedy. I took a couple of tentative steps, then spotted Sergio. He'd moved to lane 3 and was heading right toward me. I sped up and stuck out my hand.

Smack! The baton landed squarely in my palm, and I never broke stride. The Eastside guy was a half-meter ahead of me, and a runner in blue was beside him. We were in fifth, but the leader wasn't way out there at all.

I heard my name from every direction: Adam, Tanya, Coach, Javon. I sprinted all-out for the first turn, trying not to lose ground. Then I finally started to think.

Pace! That was the key. I settled down slightly and watched the Eastside runner's back. No need to pass him yet. Stay right here. We were motoring!

Click-click-click went our spikes. The baton felt light as a feather, and it helped me keep my rhythm.

Down the backstretch. We'd closed the gap on the leaders. I shifted to the outer edge of the inside lane. The runner in blue was slowing down.

I moved into fourth at the head of the turn, still keeping pace with Eastside. He'd been ahead of me until the final meters the other day. But I felt stronger than ever.

He picked up the pace as we entered the homestretch, moving out to lane 2 and passing the Kennedy runner into second. I clung tight. The Hillsdale runner was in trouble, groaning and straining in the lead.

Suddenly we were past him, neck and neck. I looked up and saw Adam straight ahead, reaching back, yelling, "Right here, Marcus!"

I lunged at the line and brought down the baton. Adam grabbed it and shot into the lead.

Two runners bumped into me as they made their exchanges. I waited till the track cleared, then hurried to the infield. Torry, Sergio, and Oscar mobbed me.

"Fifth to first!" Torry said. "You are the man!"

I was panting so hard that I couldn't talk. I stood and watched as Adam raced around the track, pulling away from the Eastside anchor but giving up ground to Hillsdale and Kennedy. It was a three-man battle now, with 200 meters to go.

I let Torry and the others do my yelling for me, but inside I was shouting. *Come on, Adam! Get us that win!*

My legs were hurting and my chest ached. But that had been the most thrilling minute of my life.

"Bethune in first, Hillsdale second, Kennedy third," the announcer said as they reached the final straightaway. "Looks like another nail-biter."

The crowd was at its loudest, with the home team pushing for a win.

But Kennedy inched ahead, then Hillsdale.

Adam fought back. With 10 meters left, they were all even.

But Adam did it. We won! And that was even more thrilling than my run. All of my exhaustion was suddenly gone, replaced by exhilaration. I leaped and raised my arms.

"Score one for the home team," said the announcer.

I glanced at the big clock at the finish line. We'd run much faster than expected. We'd broken the school record! Chalk one up to adrenaline.

The girls' teams took the track. Tanya ran over and slapped my palms. "Champions!" she said.

"You too," I said. "Make it a double."

We climbed the bleachers to join the rest of our team. The Bethune girls finished third, but Tanya ran a great anchor leg.

I found my parents, who were sitting with the Santanas. I shook hands with all of them, including Torry's little sister. But I was too excited to sit down. I felt like I could run another 400 right then.

Dad pointed to his watch. "You were about two seconds faster than in the trial," he said. "You keep getting better every time."

Two seconds might not sound like much, but it's a lot when you're going all out.

After the next event finished, the results of our race were announced. "That was Marcus Thorpe with the impressive third leg for Bethune, and Adam Hernandez on the anchor," he said after noting the top three teams.

Mom hugged me and Dad rubbed my head. I could hear my teammates yelling on the other side of the bleachers.

"Go hang out with your friends," Mom said. "Meet us here after the meet."

Dad winked at me. "Don't forget to pick up your medal," he said. "The first of many, I'm sure."

I felt like I was floating, so happy and kind of stunned by what I'd accomplished. I was also very hungry.

"Money for a snack?" I asked, holding out my hand.

"Sure," Mom said. She handed me a bill. "Treat Torry, too."

Our foursome picked up the medals, then headed for the refreshment stand. We climbed to the top row of the bleachers with our fries and sodas. I stared at my medal. It said TWILIGHT RELAYS, with a winged track shoe in the middle.

"Wish there was a fifth one for you," I said to Torry.

"Next time," he said. "I'm pointing toward the league meet for my first medal. You should, too."

That sounded like a possibility. After tonight, who knows? I'd run faster than Oscar tonight, and only about a second slower than Adam. With a few more weeks of training . . .

"Hey, Marcus," Torry said.

I looked over. He gave me a big grin and did his slow-motion running thing. "Let's call that the Bethune Shuffle," he said.

I laughed. Track is serious business, but it was good to be joking around with him again. You can't be serious all the time.

"Bethune Shuffle," I said. "Not bad. I was thinking the 'Torry Tie-Up' or the 'Marcus Collapse,' but I like your idea better. That way we can all own it."

"It happens to the best of us, right?" he said.

"The best." Yeah. I liked that.

It sounded something like me.